Sophie Johnson:
DETECTIVE
GENIUS

For Ailsa xx – MH

For my Mum – EO

SIMON & SCHUSTER
First published in Great Britain in 2019 by Simon & Schuster UK Ltd • 1st Floor, 222 Gray's Inn Road, London, WC1X 8HB • A CBS Company • Text copyright © 2019 Morag Hood • Illustrations copyright © 2019 Ella Okstad • The right of Morag Hood and Ella Okstad to be identified as the author and illustrator of this work has been asserted by them in accordance with the Copyright, Designs and Patents Act, 1988 • All rights reserved, including the right of reproduction in whole or in part in any form • A CIP catalogue record for this book is available from the British Library upon request.
978-1-4711-4564-3 (HB) • 978-1-4711-4565-0 (PB) • 978-1-4711-4566-7 (eBook)
Printed in China • 10 9 8 7 6 5 4 3 2 1

Sophie Johnson: DETECTIVE GENIUS

Morag Hood and Ella Okstad

SIMON & SCHUSTER

London   New York   Sydney   Toronto   New Delhi

My name is
Sophie Johnson
and I am a
detective genius.

DETECTIVE PARTY!

SECRETS VOL III

FAMOUS SPIES

MAKING TRAPS

CLUES VOL V

WOMEN DETECTIVES

MORSE CODE

UNDER COVER

I solve crimes and battle baddies.
And I sometimes eat my vegetables.

I had to study really hard to
learn how to be a detective,

but luckily,

I knew where to look.

This is my new assistant, Bella.

She's not a very good assistant, actually.

We are the same age,

but I am definitely smarter than her.

Bella's not very keen on detecting outdoors . . .

and she's a very fussy eater.

But I don't have time to teach Bella
how to be a detective . . .

. . . I have a lot of Very Important Things to be doing.

There has been a terrible crime, and I, Sophie Johnson: Detective Genius will find out who the criminal is!

I get straight to work, arresting suspects and taking fingerprints, but Bella doesn't understand what being a detective is all about.

She just keeps trying to show me things
that I know can't possibly be important.

While I am very busy detecting things,

Bella just shouts about nothing all day long.

She is always pestering me to play silly games with her, but I won't be distracted. I have interviews to do.

I SPY
CLUES VOL II
CLUES VOL I
DETECTIVES

Catching criminals doesn't happen
without a lot of hard work, you know . . .

. . . and Bella is no help,

no help at all.

Bella wouldn't notice if a crime happened

right under her nose.

Really, it's a good job I'm here, otherwise there would be criminals **everywhere**.

That's why they need me –
Sophie Johnson, Detective Genius.